On Thin Ice

Table of Contents

Chapter 1

"I got this medal for best short ice-skating routine," Emma Stavros told the group of fourth-grade girls who were gathered around her on the Cherrydale Elementary School playground.

Katie Carew stared at the big gold medal Emma S. was wearing around her neck. "Isn't that heavy?" she asked.

Emma S. nodded. "Yeah. But I love wearing it. I was up against some pretty tough competition. One girl was even a sixth-grader. But she couldn't land her axel the way I could. It's a jump. You start on the outside of your left foot and . . ."

Katie didn't get to hear the rest of Emma S.'s explanation, because her best friend, Suzanne Lock, pulled her away from the crowd.

"Can you believe Emma S.?" Suzanne asked Katie. "She brags so much. I mean, I've been in lots of runway shows in my modeling class, but you don't see *me* walking around with a medal around my neck."

Katie had a feeling that if Suzanne *had* a gold medal, she would definitely be wearing it. But she didn't say that. Suzanne would just deny it, anyway.

"I don't see what the big deal is about ice-skating, anyway," Suzanne went on. "It's just sliding around the ice. Anyone can do it."

Katie shook her head. "Not the way Emma S. can. I've seen her. She's amazing."

"Modeling is much harder," Suzanne told Katie. "I doubt Emma S. could walk down a runway in high heels without falling.

No one in this grade *besides me*—could ever be a model."

Katie shrugged. "No one in this grade besides Emma S. could win a gold medal in a skating competition, either. People have different talents."

Suzanne sighed. "Yeah, well, she doesn't have to brag so much about it."

Katie choked back a laugh. That was pretty funny coming from Suzanne. After all, if they gave medals for bragging, Suzanne would be the world champion!

"And guess what!" Katie heard Emma S. say. "You guys aren't going to believe *this*."

Katie turned her attention away from Suzanne and moved closer so she could hear what Emma S. was saying.

"Kerry Gaffigan is coming to town this Sunday!" Emma S. squealed. "She's going to put on a special show at the Cherrydale Arena!"

That was exciting! Kerry Gaffigan was a

very famous skater. Even Katie—who knew almost nothing about ice-skating—had heard of her.

Kerry had grown up in Cherrydale. She had learned to skate at the same rink where Emma S. skated now. Kerry was so talented, she'd even skated in the Olympics!

"Kerry Gaffigan!" Mandy Banks exclaimed. "Wow!"

"I know," Emma S. said. "She's totally my hero. And I'm going to get to meet her."

"Yeah, right," Suzanne said, rolling her eyes. "How are *you* going to meet an Olympic skater?"

"Anyone can—if you have a ticket to the show," Emma S. told her. "She's signing autographs before her performance."

"Oh, so it's not like you're the only one who's going to meet her," Suzanne said. "You'll probably have to wait in line for hours."

Emma S. shrugged. "I don't care, as long as

I get her autograph."

"Oh, I want to go, too," Miriam said. "Do you think there are tickets left?"

Emma S. nodded. "Sure. The kids who skate at the rink got first dibs, but the rest of you can get tickets after school."

"Oh, wow!" Emma Weber exclaimed. She turned to Katie. "We're going to meet a real live Olympic athlete."

"I'm definitely going. Do you want a ticket for the show?" Katie asked Suzanne.

Suzanne sighed. "If I don't have anything better to do, I might," she said. "Of course, I might have to go to New York or Paris for a modeling show that day."

"Wow," Emma W. said. "I didn't know you were modeling professionally now."

Suzanne frowned slightly. "Well, I'm not, exactly. But you never know. Maybe someone will come to my modeling class this afternoon and discover me."

Katie sighed. That was a really big *maybe*!

"Now all we're going to hear about is this stupid skating show," Suzanne groaned. "I wish Emma S. had just kept her mouth shut."

"No you don't!" Katie shouted loudly at her. "You don't wish that at all!"

Suzanne stared at Katie with surprise. "I didn't say anything so bad," she said.

Katie could see that Suzanne thought she

was nuts for getting so upset. But Suzanne *had* said something bad—*really* bad.

And only Katie knew why.

Chapter 2

It all started one horrible day back in third grade. Katie had lost the football game for her team. Then she'd splashed mud all over her favorite jeans. But the worst part of the day came when Katie let out a loud burp—right in front of the whole class. Talk about embarrassing!

That night, Katie wished to be anyone but herself. There must have been a shooting star overhead when she made the wish, because the very next day the magic wind came.

The magic wind was like a really powerful tornado that blew only around Katie. It was so strong, it could blow her right out of her body *. . . and into someone else's!*

The first time the magic wind appeared, it turned Katie into Speedy, the hamster in her third-grade class. Katie spent the whole morning going round and round on a hamster wheel and chewing on Speedy's wooden chew sticks. And that wasn't even the worst part. Things got *really* bad when she escaped from Speedy's cage and ran into the boys' locker room. That was when Katie landed inside George Brennan's stinky sneaker! *Pee-yew!* Katie sure was glad when the magic wind came back and switcherooed her into herself again!

After that, the magic wind came back again and again. Sometimes it changed Katie into other kids. One time it turned her into Suzanne. Another time it turned her into Suzanne's baby sister!

And when the magic wind switcherooed her into their school principal, Mr. Kane, there was chaos at the school. By the end of the day, kids were running wild in the halls, and all the electricity had gone out in the building.

The magic wind followed Katie every-where—even to Europe! In Spain, the magic wind turned Katie into a flamenco dancer in a Spanish restaurant. Katie was not a very good dancer. She'd fallen off the stage, landed in some man's lap, and sent rice and lobster claws flying all over the place! *Ay, caramba*!

The magic wind was the reason Katie hated wishes so much. They only brought trouble. But she couldn't explain that to Suzanne. She wouldn't believe her, anyway. Katie wouldn't have believed it, either, if it didn't keep happening to her.

"I know you didn't say anything so bad," Katie told Suzanne finally. "It's just that when you say things like that, you sound kind of jealous. And I know that's not true," she added quickly.

"I'm *never* jealous," Suzanne said. "Other people are jealous of *me*."

"Of course they are," Katie said, trying really hard not to laugh. Suzanne never changed. Suzanne was always Suzanne.

Except, of course, for that time when *Katie* had been Suzanne.

Chapter 3

Today was Katie's favorite school day. That was because Wednesday was class 4A's library day. Each week the kids got to pick out a new library book to take home.

"Do you have any more books by Nellie Farrow?" Katie asked Ms. Folio, the school librarian.

"I knew you were going to ask me that, Katie," Ms. Folio said. "The new one just came in. I put it away for you."

Katie grinned. It was amazing. There were so many kids at Cherrydale Elementary School, and Ms. Folio was able to remember what every kid loved to read.

"Emma W., here's a book about a big sister with a little brother who is a real trouble-maker," Ms. Folio said, handing her a fat chapter book.

Emma W. smiled. "I can relate to that," she said.

Katie knew exactly what Emma W. meant. Emma W. had *three* little brothers—*and* an older sister!

"This book is full of really funny library jokes," Ms. Folio told Kadeem, handing him a paperback book.

"Hey, that's not fair! I want a joke book, too," George shouted out.

Katie sighed. She'd been expecting that. George and Kadeem were always having joke-telling contests against one another.

"Don't get upset," Ms. Folio told George. "I have a really special book for you. It's a biography of Harry Houdini, the greatest magician who ever lived."

"But I don't know anything about magic,"

George said with a shrug.

"You will after you read the book," Ms. Folio told him.

"Hey, you guys, this joke is sooo funny," Kadeem said, looking up from the joke book. "Why was the Tyrannosaurus rex afraid to go to the library?"

"Why?" Andy Epstein asked him.

"Because his book was six million years overdue!" Kadeem said with a laugh.

The other kids laughed, too.

"Oh yeah?" George butted in. "Well, how can you tell if an elephant checked out a library book before you did?"

"How?" Kevin asked him.

"When you open the cover, peanut shells fall out!" George exclaimed.

Everyone laughed again.

"See? I don't need a joke book to make *me* funny," George told Kadeem.

But Kadeem wasn't scared off. He turned the page of his book and grinned. "Here's a good one," he told the kids. "What goes on a librarian's fishing hook?"

"A bookworm!" George shouted out before Kadeem could say the punch line. "That's an old one."

"Okay, dudes," Mr. G., Katie's teacher, said, stepping between the boys. "Let's put this joke-off *off* until later. There are still a few people who don't have books yet, and we don't have much library time left."

"Speaking of which," Ms. Folio said,

handing Emma S. a thick book. "Here's a biography of Kerry Gaffigan for you to read, Emma. I hear she's coming to town this weekend."

Emma S. nodded. "On Sunday. And I'm going to meet her. This book is absolutely perfect for me. Now I won't just be Kerry's biggest fan, I'll be the world's greatest expert on her, too."

Katie sighed. She was glad Suzanne wasn't around to hear that.

Chapter 4

"Does anyone have a nickel?" George asked the crowd of kids who had gathered around him on the school playground the next day at recess.

"I have one," Jeremy Fox said. He handed his nickel to George.

Jeremy was Katie's other best friend. "Careful, Jeremy," she warned. "George is learning magic. He might make your nickel disappear."

"No I won't," George insisted. "In fact, I'm going to make this nickel grow into a quarter."

"That's impossible, George," Suzanne told him.

"The Great Georgini can do anything!" George exclaimed.

"This I've gotta see," Suzanne scoffed.

George took Jeremy's nickel and placed it in a small, red, rectangular plastic box. He shut the box and waved his hand over it. "Abracadabra!" he said in his best magician's voice.

The kids all watched as George opened the box once again. "Ta-da!" George shouted.

Katie's eyes opened wide as she looked in the open box. Sure enough, the nickel had become a quarter. "Wow! That is so cool, Great Georgini!" she exclaimed.

"Thank you, Katie Kazoo," George said with a bow.

Katie grinned. She loved the way-cool nickname George had given her back in third grade.

"You should try that with dollar bills," Mandy told George. "You could be a million-aire."

"It only works with nickels and quarters," George explained.

"Speaking of nickels," Jeremy reminded him. "Can I have mine back?"

"Yeah, sure," George said. He closed the little box, waved his hand over it, and said, "Abracadabra!" When he opened the box again, the nickel was back in place.

"Can you teach me how to do that?" Andy asked him.

The Great Georgini shook his head. "A magician never reveals his secrets."

"Then how did *you* learn the trick?" Suzanne asked him.

"They're *illusions*, not tricks," George corrected her. "That's what Harry Houdini called them. My parents bought me a magic kit at the mall yesterday. The secret was in the instruction book."

"You sure learned it well," Katie told him.

"You guys want to see another illusion?" George asked.

But before anyone could answer, Emma S. came running over. She had a big envelope in her hand. "I have invitations for everyone," she said as she began handing out ice-skate-shaped pieces of paper.

"Invitations to what?" Emma W. asked.

"My ice-skating party," Emma S. explained. "It's on Saturday at the Cherrydale Rink. My parents are throwing me a party for getting the gold medal. They said I can invite the whole grade. It's going to be great. We can skate for a whole hour. Then we're going to have hot cocoa and cookies!"

"This is perfect!" Miriam squealed. "We can watch you skate on Saturday and Kerry Gaffigan skate on Sunday. My mom picked up my ticket yesterday afternoon."

"So did mine!" Katie exclaimed.

"Mine too," Emma W. chimed in.

Emma S. nodded. "It will be a super skating weekend!"

The kids seemed really psyched about that.

All except Suzanne. She didn't seem to think the idea of a skating weekend was super at all.

"She's just having this party so she can show off," Suzanne whispered to Katie.

Katie shrugged. "Maybe she can show us how to do some easy tricks," she suggested.

"Why would I want to learn that?" Suzanne said. "I hate skating. The ice is cold, and it hurts."

"Ice *hurts*?" Katie asked, confused.

"When you fall on it, it does," Suzanne said. "Not that *I* fall when I skate or anything. I'm too graceful for that. Models are *always* graceful."

"Of course," Katie said, trying not to laugh. "*I* fall a lot, though. I'm hoping Emma S. will give me a few tips."

"If it means she can show off, she will," Suzanne said.

"So are you going to the party?" Katie asked. From the way Suzanne was acting, it sure didn't seem that way.

"Yeah, I'll go," Suzanne said reluctantly. She stood quietly for a minute. Then a strange little smile began to form on her lips. "Come to think of it, this party could turn out to be kind of fun."

Katie frowned. She didn't like the sound of that. Suzanne was definitely planning something. But what?

Chapter 5

"Suzanne, are you walking home?" Katie asked as she walked out of the school at the end of the day.

Suzanne nodded. "But I'm waiting to talk to George first."

Katie looked at her strangely. Suzanne never waited for George. She *hated* George. What was this all about?

It didn't take Katie long to find out. A moment later, George came bounding down the steps with Kevin at his side.

"Hey, Katie Kazoo, you've gotta see George's new illusion," Kevin said. "It's amazing."

"Show it to us, George," Suzanne said excitedly.

Kevin, George, and Katie all stared at her.

"Aw, go away, Suzanne," George groaned.

"No. I want to see it," Suzanne told him. "Honest."

George looked at her as if he was waiting to make sure she wasn't making fun of him.

Katie was wondering the same thing. But Suzanne really did look interested in George's trick.

"Okay, so I start with these regular dice," George said. He handed the two dice to Katie. "Katie Kazoo, please check them out and assure everyone that they're completely normal."

Katie studied the two plastic cubes. They looked like regular playing dice. They were white, with dots on every side. "Yep. Just everyday dice," she said.

"Now I place the dice into the magic box," George continued, putting the dice into a square box and closing the lid. "Then you say the magic words . . ."

"Abracadabra!" Katie, Suzanne, and Kevin shouted together.

George opened the box. There were two dice in there, all right. But they were completely blank.

"Whoa! Amazing!" Kevin exclaimed.

"Incredible," Katie agreed.

"It's okay . . ." Suzanne said slowly.

"Just okay?" Kevin asked. "Are you nuts? The Great Georgini is an awesome magician."

"He's pretty good," Suzanne told him. "But I know how he could be better."

"Of course you do," George said sarcastically.

"No, I'm serious," Suzanne told him. "Your trick was really good. You're just missing something."

"What?" George asked angrily.

"You need an assistant in a pretty sequined dress," Suzanne said.

Katie sighed. So that was what this was all about.

"The Great Georgini doesn't need an assistant," Kevin told her.

"Sure he does," Suzanne insisted. "Houdini had an assistant, didn't he, George?"

George nodded. "He had a few of them."

"Well, you only need one," Suzanne continued. "And I know just the perfect person to do it. Me!"

"You?" George, Katie, and Kevin all asked at once.

"Sure," Suzanne said. "I'll make your act classier. And you'll be more like Houdini."

"Well . . ." George began.

"Great!" Suzanne exclaimed before George could say no. "Let's go to your house right now and practice."

"I . . . uh . . ." George stammered. "Okay. I guess."

Suzanne smiled triumphantly. "We're going to make a great team. Suzanne Superstar and the Great Georgini."

"You mean the Great Georgini and his assistant, Suzanne," George corrected her.

Suzanne shrugged. "We can discuss that later. Right now we have an act to put together."

Just then, Jessica Haynes, Mandy, Miriam,

and Emma S. walked out of the school building. They were all talking very excitedly.

"I'm going to wear my blue skating outfit," Emma S. said. "It's brand-new. And wait until you see the silver beads on the skirt!"

"Remember, you promised to show us how to skate backward," Mandy told Emma S.

"Definitely," Emma S. agreed. "And I'll show you how to spin after that."

"This is going to be the best party ever!" Jessica squealed.

"It sure is," Suzanne interrupted.

Everyone stared at her in shock.

"No, I mean it," Suzanne insisted. "A skating party is a great idea. And it's about to get even better!"

"What are you talking about, Suzanne?" Emma S. asked suspiciously.

"I'm talking about the special entertainment you're going to have while people are having cocoa and cookies," Suzanne continued.

"*What* entertainment?" Emma S. asked her.

"The Great Georgini, and his amazing assistant, Suzanne Superstar!" Suzanne exclaimed.

"What? Suzanne . . ." George began, shaking his head.

"It will be fun," Suzanne insisted.

Katie sighed. So that was what Suzanne had been cooking up. She'd found a way to make herself the star of Emma S.'s party. Suzanne really *was* amazing!

"It *would* be nice to have a show while we eat," Emma S. agreed.

"What other tricks will you do?" Jessica asked George.

"Well, I . . ." George stammered. "I don't know that many yet and . . ."

"That's why we're leaving now," Suzanne said, pulling George by the arm. "The Great Georgini and I are about to put together the world's most amazing magic act!"

Katie frowned as George and Suzanne walked away. Poor George. He'd gotten caught up in one Suzanne's crazy schemes.

That was *so* not good.

Chapter 6

"You've gotta hide me, Katie Kazoo," George said as he hurried to catch up to Jeremy and Katie as they walked to the playground at recess on Friday.

"Hide you from what?" Katie asked him curiously.

"From Suzanne," George said. "She's making me nuts."

"You could go hang out in the boys' bathroom," Jeremy suggested.

"Yeah, Suzanne can't get you in there," Katie agreed.

"I've done that before," Jeremy said. "To get away from Becky."

Katie nodded with understanding. Becky had a big crush on Jeremy. She was always following him around and flirting with him. Jeremy did *not* flirt back . . . at all!

"But I don't want to spend my whole recess in the bathroom," George said.

Just then, the three kids heard someone yelling across the playground. "Great Georgini! Are you ready to rehearse?"

George groaned at the sound of Suzanne's loud voice. "Hanging out with the sinks and toilets would be better than spending recess with her," he said as he ran back into the school building.

"Where did George go?" Suzanne asked Katie and Jeremy as she caught up to them near the big tree.

"Bathroom," Jeremy said.

"Oh," Suzanne said. "Well, I'll just wait for him, I guess."

"You'll be waiting a long time," Jeremy told her.

"Why?" Suzanne asked.

"He . . . um . . . he said his stomach was bothering him or something," Katie said quickly. She didn't want Suzanne's feelings to be hurt.

"Oh, something's bothering him all right," Jeremy laughed. He looked straight at Suzanne.

"Why don't we go play double Dutch jump rope?" Katie asked, pulling Suzanne away before Jeremy could say anything else. "George can find you when he comes out."

"I guess," Suzanne said with a shrug.

A few moments later, Katie and Suzanne were part of the big group of girls who were playing double Dutch jump rope. Emma W. was jumping and singing a rhyme about a teddy bear.

Ordinarily, the other girls would be chanting along with her. But today it seemed that none of the girls could focus on the game. They were all too excited.

"This is going to be such a great weekend,"
Miriam said. "The party, and the show . . ."

"Oh, the show's going to be amazing,"
Suzanne told her. "George and I have worked
up some great tricks."

"I meant Kerry Gaffigan's ice show,"
Miriam explained.

"Oh," Suzanne said with a shrug. "Yeah, I
guess that will be good, too."

Katie sighed.

"Your turn, Becky," Emma W. said as she

stepped on the rope and lost her turn.

"Okay," Becky said, jumping into the ropes. As her feet moved up and down on the pavement, she began singing her rhyme. "Raspberry, blueberry, apple tart. Tell me the name of my sweetheart. Is it A, B, C . . ."

Katie watched as Becky jumped up and down. She really was an amazing double Dutch jumper. She hardly ever missed.

Until now . . .

"G . . . H . . . I . . . *J*!" Becky shouted. "Oops," she added as she stepped on one of the ropes.

"You *soooo* did that on purpose," Jessica laughed. "You wanted to land on *J* for Jeremy."

"I did not miss on purpose," Becky insisted. "It was just fate. I guess Jeremy really is my sweetheart!" She looked around the yard. "Oooh. There he is, on the soccer field. Yoohoo! Jeremy! Wait until I tell you what just happened."

At the sound of Becky's voice, Jeremy started to run! And Katie knew just where he was heading . . .

To spend recess with George—in the boys' bathroom.

Chapter 7

"Okay, so to skate backward, start with your toes touching and your heels facing out, sort of like an upside-down V," Emma S. told Katie, Jessica, Miriam, and Emma W. during her skating party the next day. "Then bend your knees and slide your heels together to make a right-side-up V. Just keep making Vs like that over and over, and you'll move backward."

That doesn't sound so hard, Katie thought as she placed her toes together on the ice and tried to follow Emma S.'s instructions.

But skating backward was a lot harder than it sounded.

Flop! Katie landed right on her backside.

Emma S. smiled as she reached down to help Katie up. "Almost," she assured her. "Maybe you should hold onto the wall with one hand until you really have it under control."

"Good idea," Katie said, trying not to think about how much her wet rear end stung. She reached over and grabbed the top of the low wall with her right hand.

"Is this it?" Miriam asked as she zigzagged her feet and began slowly moving backward.

"Uh-huh," Emma S. said. "Now see if you can speed it up."

But Miriam had stopped listening. She was too busy looking out at the ice. "I didn't know Jeremy could skate that fast," she pointed out.

Katie turned her head just as Jeremy whizzed by. Boy, he was really flying around the ice.

It didn't take long to figure out why. A minute later, Becky skated past as well.

"Jeremy, wait up!" Becky shouted to him. "I want to see if you can lift me up in the air, like the ice dancers do on TV."

Katie frowned. Poor Jeremy. There was just no escaping Becky.

She put her toes together in an upside-down V, and tried once again to slide her feet backward. A few more tries, and suddenly she felt herself moving in reverse. Sure, she was going slowly, and she was still grabbing onto the wall a little bit, but she was definitely skating backward.

"Yes!" Katie shouted, pumping her fist in the air. She sure was happy Emma S. had put together this skating party. Skating was great—if you didn't mind falling every now and then.

Too bad Suzanne and George were missing all the fun. They were busy inside the café, setting up their magic show.

× × ×

A little while later, the kids were all nice and warm inside the rink's café, sipping hot cocoa, and watching the Great Georgini work his magic.

"I will now stick this ordinary sewing needle into a balloon. But the balloon will not pop!" George boasted.

Suzanne smiled at the crowd and held a bright red balloon in the air. Then she twirled around, showing off her glittery pink leotard and skirt.

"Abracadabra, pop no more!" George shouted as he slowly stuck the needle into the balloon.

Katie covered her ears. She hated the sound of balloons popping. And somehow, she didn't think George would be able to stop that from happening. He wasn't *that* good a magician.

Or was he? The balloon didn't pop! It stayed round and full!

"Wow!" Katie shouted. She clapped really hard.

"Awesome!" Jeremy cheered.

"Go, Georgini!" Kevin chimed in.

"Hey, you guys ever hear the joke about the balloon and the tree . . ." Kadeem called out, interrupting the applause.

"Not now, Kadeem," Miriam told him. "George is about to do another trick."

"But this joke's really funny," Kadeem insisted.

"Save it for the next joke-off at school," Kevin suggested.

Kadeem frowned and sat back in his chair. He looked kind of upset. Katie understood why. Kadeem and George were always competing for attention. That's why they had all those joke-offs. But Kadeem couldn't compete with George today. George knew magic and Kadeem didn't.

"Watch now as I pour water on this tissue," George said in a deep, magician-like voice. "And yet, thanks to my magic skills, the tissue will remain completely dry."

"He will do it all with *my* help!" Suzanne added, jumping in front of George and whirling around in her sparkly costume as she placed two large plastic cups and a pitcher of water on the table.

George pointed to one of the two large plastic cups. "I will now place this ordinary tissue into this cup," he said, holding up a yellow tissue. "And then I will pour water from this pitcher into the cup. But the tissue won't get wet at all."

"Impossible," Andy said.

"Is it real water?" Kevin asked.

"I'll drink some to prove it," Suzanne said, picking up a cup and starting to pour herself a drink.

"Not that cup, Suzanne," George warned her.

"Why n—" Suzanne stopped herself. "Oh, yeah, right. That one has the smaller cup glued inside it."

"The *what*?" Kadeem asked.

George glared at Suzanne. "I can't believe you said that!" he shouted at her.

"But I . . ." Suzanne began. She bit her lip. "It just slipped out."

"You gave away how the illusion is done!" George shouted. "A magician is never sup-posed to do that."

Kadeem jumped up and grabbed the cup. "Check it out!" he shouted to the kids. "There's a little cup glued to the inside of the big one. George was going to put the tissue in

the little cup. Then he could pour the water into the big cup without getting any in the little one." Kadeem began to laugh. "That's how the trick works!"

George's cheeks got beet red. "I'm finished with magic!" he shouted as he turned and ran out of the café.

Suddenly Kadeem looked really sorry. He had definitely gotten the last laugh that time. But Katie could tell he hadn't meant to make George feel *that* bad.

Suzanne looked pretty upset, too. She stood there for a minute not knowing what to do. Then she spun around again. "That's the great Georgini's best trick," she told the crowd. "He made himself disappear!"

The kids all started to laugh. All but Katie, that is. She went after George.

"George, please don't let Kadeem and Suzanne upset you," Katie urged him.

"Suzanne always ruins everything!" George said. "And she's always butting her nose in where she doesn't belong."

Katie didn't know what to say to that. Sometimes there was no defending Suzanne.

"Don't let her stop your show," Katie urged George, finally. "Come back and do the rest of your tricks."

"They're *illusions*!" George insisted. "I keep telling everyone that!"

"Okay. Come do your illusions, then."

George shook his head. "No way. I'm finished with magic . . . forever!"

Chapter 8

"Your party was really awesome," Miriam told Emma S. the next morning. "Even with George's awful magic show."

"Thanks," Emma S. replied. "I had a great time, too. But nothing beats this. I can't believe I'm five people away from meeting Kerry Gaffigan!"

Katie couldn't believe it, either. She was only *seven* people away—just behind Emma S. and Miriam. Emma W. was behind Katie. Suzanne was all the way in the back of the line.

That meant Suzanne was going to be waiting a long time to meet Kerry. It seemed like there were a hundred girls in line. And they were all holding gifts for Kerry. Some, like Emma S. and Miriam, had little teddy bears for her. A few, like Katie, were holding bunches of flowers.

But Katie was sure her flowers were the best. Most of the other girls were holding different colored carnations. But Katie hadn't wanted anything that ordinary for Kerry Gaffigan. She and her mom had stopped at the Flower Power Flower Shop in the Cherrydale Mall early that morning. Katie had picked out a bouquet of the reddest roses she could find.

The line kept moving. One by one, each girl in line had a few minutes to speak to Kerry. The skater was already in the Snow White costume and black wig she was going to wear for the first half of the show.

Katie listened as the kids ahead of her talked to Kerry. Some of the girls asked her questions about skating. Some asked her questions about her childhood. One teenager even asked her about her boyfriend—a professional snowboarder named Tony Raven. Kerry blushed a little at that question.

"She looks beautiful," Emma S. said to Katie, Miriam, and Emma W. "Kerry's Snow White ice-skating routine is so awesome. She skates with these guys who are dressed as dwarfs and everything. I saw her do it on TV once."

Just then, the girl in front of Emma S. finished talking to Kerry. "Oh my gosh. It's my turn to meet Kerry Gaffigan," Emma S. gasped as her cheeks turned red with excitement.

Katie watched as Emma walked up to the table and stared at her idol. She'd never seen anyone so excited.

"Kerry Gaffigan!" Emma S. squealed nervously. "Do you know who you are?"

Oops. That definitely wasn't one of the questions Emma had meant to ask.

A few of the girls in line giggled. But Kerry Gaffigan didn't laugh at all. Instead, she smiled kindly. "I sure hope I do," she told Emma S. gently. "But I don't know who *you* are. What's your name?"

Kerry's cheerful voice seemed to calm Emma down. "I'm Emma Stavros," she answered her. "I'm a skater. I want to be just like you!"

Emma S. and Kerry chatted for a while about skating moves—at least that's what Katie figured camels, lutzes, and toe loops were. Then Emma moved away from the line, clutching her autographed skating bag.

Miriam was the next to talk to Kerry. "I just learned to skate backward. Emma taught me," she said.

Kerry turned her head and smiled at Emma S. "That was very kind of Emma," she said.

Emma S. heard and looked as if she was about to fly up in the air and do a triple spin. She was that proud and excited.

"I am so glad you are beginning to

ice skate," Kerry said as she signed a page in Miriam's autograph book. "Good luck."

And then it was Katie's turn! Katie could feel her heart thump-thump-thumping as she walked up to the table. She didn't know what to say. It was hard to talk to someone as famous as Kerry Gaffigan.

"H-H-Hi!" Katie stammered. "I'm Katie. And these are for you." She thrust forward the bouquet of red, red roses.

Katie had expected Kerry to give her a big smile and thank her for the most beautiful roses she had ever seen. But . . .

"Roses! No!" Kerry shouted, pushing away the bouquet and jumping up from the table. "Get those away!"

"But . . . I . . ." Katie stammered, not quite sure what to do or say.

"Oh, no!" Kerry exclaimed. "I've got rose pollen on me. I can feel the itching starting." She began scratching at her arms. "My right eye is getting puffy. I have to take my contact

lenses out right away!" She started to cough loudly. "Sorry, I have to go."

All the girls in line stared in horror as Kerry ran off.

"How could you bring her roses?" a tall girl with glasses demanded. "*Everyone* knows Kerry Gaffigan is allergic to roses."

Katie bit her lip. Not *everyone*.

"Now we'll never get to meet Kerry," a small girl in a blue and white skating costume said. She burst into tears.

"Thanks a lot," a chubby girl in a green parka said sarcastically to Katie.

Katie didn't know what to do. She just knew she couldn't stay here with everyone yelling at her. She turned and ran away.

A few minutes later, Katie found herself all alone in a corner behind the ice rink. Katie was glad for that. She felt bad enough about making Kerry itchy and puffy without all the other kids blaming her for it. It was better to be here alone.

Suddenly, Katie felt a cool breeze blowing on the back of her neck. At first she thought it was coming from the ice.

But ice wasn't windy. It was just cold.

And ice didn't spin around like a tornado, the way this wind was starting to do.

Uh-oh! Katie gulped. This was no ordinary wind. This was the magic wind!

The magic wind grew stronger, circling wildly around Katie like a fierce tornado. It picked up speed, blowing harder and harder.

Whoosh! Katie was sure it would blow her away. She shut her eyes tight and tried not to cry.

And then it stopped. Just like that. The magic wind was gone. And so was Katie Carew.

She'd turned into somebody else. One, two, switcheroo!

But who?

Chapter 9

Katie struggled to open her eyes. That was weird. Usually her eyes would just fly open after the magic wind disappeared. But today they seemed kind of stuck and itchy.

In fact, Katie was itchy everywhere. Her arms itched. Her face itched. Her *teeth* itched—and that wasn't even possible!

Katie looked down. Everything seemed really blurry. She could just about make out the shoes on her feet. They were not the brown and white boots she had been wearing. *These* shoes were white on the top and shiny on the bottom.

Wait a minute. Those weren't shoes. Those were *skates*!

Yikes! Katie gulped nervously. If she was wearing skates, that could only mean one thing!

The magic wind had turned her into one of the skaters in the show!

"Kerry! Are you okay?" a tall man said, running over and helping Katie to her feet.

Kerry?

Double yikes! Katie wasn't just one of the skaters. The magic wind had turned her into Kerry Gaffigan!

"Um, yeah, I'm okay," Katie said, standing up. She scratched at her arm and her cheek. She wanted to scratch other places, but she figured that wouldn't be polite.

"Okay, good," the man told her. "It's one minute till showtime."

Showtime?

"But I stink at skating!" Katie shouted.

"What do you mean you stink?" the man insisted.

Oops. That was something a ten-year-old

girl would say, not an Olympic skater. "I mean, um, well, I don't have my contact lenses in, so I can't see. And I'm all itchy. So I won't be able to skate . . . *today*."

"What am I supposed to tell all the people out there?" the man asked angrily. "They're waiting to see you skate."

Katie could hear the audience rustling around in their seats. They sounded very excited. How could Katie disappoint all of Kerry's fans? She would have to go out on the ice and put on a show.

Even though she couldn't stop scratching.

Even though she couldn't see anything.

Even though *she couldn't ice skate*!

Katie gulped. This was soooo not good!

Chapter 10

Katie was so nervous, it felt like her stomach was doing spins and axels. As the music started, she squinted and tried to see what was happening on the ice. From what she could make out, a skater dressed as the evil queen was twirling around a huge cardboard and foil mirror.

"Kerry, go. You're supposed to be out there," a skater in a dwarf costume whispered to Katie.

This was it. Katie was going to have to go out there and skate.

Somehow.

Slowly, she skated out onto the ice. One

foot in front of the other. Right. Left. Right. Left. Her ankles wobbled. She held her breath and tried not to fall.

The kids in the audience cheered at the very sight of Kerry Gaffigan. Katie reached up one arm and tried to wave.

Whoops. She almost lost her balance. *Okay. No more waving. Just skating,* Katie thought. Right. Left. Right. Left.

"What are you doing?" the evil queen said under her breath. "Where's the waltz jump you were supposed to do?"

Katie didn't answer. What could she say?

Just then, the seven dwarfs skated out onto the ice. They weaved in and out between the huge cardboard trees that had been set up on the ice to make it look like a forest.

One of the dwarfs raced over to Katie, and before she knew it, he lifted her off the ground. He began to spin.

"Whoa!" Katie shouted as the dwarf twirled faster and faster. "I'm getting dizzy."

But the dwarf kept on spinning. And even after he finally set her down, Katie still felt like everything was whirling around and around. Her stomach was woozy. All she could do was stand and blink. She was afraid that if she moved, she would throw up!

Still, she *had* to skate. The audience had come expecting to watch Kerry Gaffigan on ice.

But the only ice-skating trick Katie knew was skating backward. Sort of, anyway.

Katie made an upside-down V with her feet. Then she made a right-side-up V. Then an upside-down V.

Hey! What do you know? Katie was gliding backward! She smiled and glanced up at the audience.

The faces in the crowd looked like they were waiting for a big trick. But Katie knew that wasn't going to happen.

This is it, guys, she felt like saying as she continued skating backward.

"Hey, Kerry!" one of the dwarfs suddenly shouted in Katie's direction. "I mean, Snow White. Watch out!"

Rip! Katie heard a tearing sound. It took her a moment to realize what had happened.

Oh, no! She had skated right through the silver foil mirror.

The audience grew quiet. It seemed as if everybody was holding their breath.

Katie turned around quickly to see what had happened to the mirror.

Wham!

Katie bashed right into one of the dwarfs and knocked him to the ground.

The audience gasped.

"I'm so sorry," Katie apologized to the dwarf. She reached out her hand to help him up. The skater in the dwarf costume took her hand, but Katie slipped.

"Whoa!" Katie shouted out as she landed hard on her rear end.

The audience began to boo. This was not

the kind of show they had come to see.

Katie tried to pull herself up onto her feet. But instead she started to slide. As she slid across the ice on her bottom, she knocked down one cardboard tree. Which knocked over the next cardboard tree. Which knocked over the next. And the next . . .

"Somebody help!" Katie screamed.

A few of the dwarfs raced to her rescue. Quickly, they bent down and scooted Katie off the ice.

It was scary being carried up in the air. The dwarfs were skating so fast. Katie was sure she was going to fall again.

"AAAHHHH!" she screamed as she kicked her arms and legs in the air. "AAAHHHH!"

Chapter 11

"What happened out there?" the skater who played the evil queen demanded as the dwarfs put Katie back on the ground backstage.

"Yeah, Kerry. Was that some kind of joke?" one of the dwarfs asked.

"'Cause it wasn't funny," another dwarf added.

"What were you thinking?" a third dwarf asked her.

Katie could feel tears welling up in her eyes. She was going to start crying, she just knew it.

"Um . . . I gotta go," Katie said. And she

hobbled off on her skates, searching for a quiet place to have a really good cry.

A few moments later, Katie found herself all alone in the Cherrydale Arena locker room. She sat down on a bench and rested her head in her hands. She couldn't believe what had just happened.

The magic wind had done some really rotten things before, but turning Katie into a professional skater with itchy skin and puffy eyes was just about the rottenest.

Then, all of a sudden, Katie felt a cold breeze blowing on her back. She turned to see if a window was open. But this was no ordinary wind. The magic wind had returned.

And Katie was very glad. She was tired of being Kerry Gaffigan.

The magic wind began whirling wildly around Katie. The tornado blew faster and faster, harder and harder.

Then it stopped. Just like that. The magic wind was gone.

Katie Kazoo was back!

So was Kerry Gaffigan. And boy, did she look confused.

Kerry blinked her eyes a few times and looked around. "How did I get in here?" she murmured.

"You . . . um . . . you wanted some time alone to think," Katie stammered vaguely.

Kerry squinted a little to get a good look at Katie's face. "It's you!" she exclaimed. "The girl with the roses."

Katie felt really bad about that. "I'm so sorry, Kerry," she said. "I didn't know you were allergic to roses. I just wanted to bring you the prettiest flowers I could find."

"It's okay." Kerry glanced down at her wet Snow White dress. "What happened to me?" Kerry asked.

"You had a couple of spills out on the ice," Katie said, not knowing how else to explain it.

"Then it really happened," Kerry said slowly. "The ripped magic mirror, the falling cardboard trees, the dwarfs carrying me off . . ."

Katie nodded sadly.

Kerry moaned and held her head in her hands.

"You'll skate better in the second half of the show," Katie assured her. "You're back to your old self now." Katie sighed. Kerry didn't know how true that really was.

Kerry shot Katie a look. "Skate? Are you kidding? I'm not going out there again."

"But you have to. Everyone's waiting for you," Katie insisted.

"Everyone's *laughing* at me," Kerry corrected her. "I'm a big joke. My career is ruined. I'll never skate again."

Katie's eyes opened wide. She couldn't believe her ears. Kerry Gaffigan giving up skating? She couldn't let that happen.

"Kerry, you can't do that to your fans!" she said.

"What fans? I just lost all of my fans," Kerry told her.

"No you didn't," Katie insisted. "Your fans still love you. They understand that you just had a bad day. They fall, too."

"Well of course *they* fall," Kerry said. "They're just beginners. It's okay to fall when you're just starting out."

"But if you quit after falling a few times, then they might, too," Katie said. "Remember my friend Emma who said she wants to be just like you?"

Kerry thought about that.

"A *lot* of girls want to be just like you," Katie continued.

Kerry didn't say anything. She just bent down and started to take off her skates.

This was bad. Katie could tell. "You're really not going to skate anymore?" she asked nervously.

Kerry shook her head. Then she grinned. "Not in these skates I'm not. I have different skates for my Alice in Wonderland costume. That's what I wear in the second act of the show."

Katie breathed a big sigh of relief. "Oh, I'm so glad!" she exclaimed.

"You're pretty smart for a kid, you know that?" Kerry said with a grin.

Katie smiled. "I'm smart enough to know I'd better get back to my seat," she told Kerry. "Because I can't wait to see you skate in person!"

Chapter 12

"Wasn't Kerry amazing as Alice in Wonderland?" Emma S. asked Katie, Emma W., and Miriam as the girls stood together on the playground the next morning.

Miriam nodded. "I loved the way she twirled when she was supposed to be falling down the rabbit hole."

"Spinning is really hard on the ice. It can make you kinda sick to your stomach," Katie added.

Emma S. looked at her curiously. "How would you know?" she asked her.

Oops. Emma S. didn't know it was actually Katie who had been spinning with that dwarf yesterday. "It *looks* like it would make you kind of queasy," Katie corrected herself. *Phew.* That was close.

Just then, George walked over to the girls. "Hey, Katie Kazoo," he said, holding out a deck of cards. "Pick a card. And don't show it to me."

Katie pulled a card from the deck and peeked at it. It was the ace of hearts. "I thought you'd given up on magic," she said.

"Well, did you read that article about Kerry Gaffigan in the newspaper this morning?" George replied. "She told the reporter that even though she had messed up part of her show, she was never going to give up on skating."

Katie grinned. She knew why Kerry had said that. But Katie didn't say anything. It didn't matter, anyway. All that mattered was that Kerry Gaffigan was still skating, and the Great Georgini was still doing his magic tricks.

Emma S. nodded. "Kerry said you had to learn from your mistakes to make yourself better."

"Right," George agreed. "And I've learned from *my* mistake. I'm never going to do a magic show with Suzanne again! From now on, the Great Georgini is a solo act."

"Good idea," Miriam said with a giggle.

George closed his eyes and looked like he was concentrating really hard. "Yes. In my

mind, I can see the card you picked, Katie."
The Great Georgini paused. "You picked the
two of hearts."

Katie shook her head. "Nope. Try again."

George fingered the cards for a minute.
"Oh, wait. It was the *ace* of hearts!"

"You got it!" Katie exclaimed happily.

"Me next," Emma S. said to George.

As Katie watched George perform his card
trick again, she smiled contentedly. It was so
nice to have things back to normal again.

Well . . . as normal as things can be when
you are always waiting for the next magic
wind to arrive.

Going Downhill

Chapter 1

"Cowabunga!" George Brennan shouted as he crouched slightly on his snowboard and took off down the big hill.

"Whoa! Check him out!" Kevin Camilleri, George's best friend, exclaimed.

"He's as good as a professional," Katie Carew said. She watched as George slid downhill faster and faster. She was sure he would fall. But he didn't. Not once.

"Come on, Katie Kazoo," Jeremy Fox, one of Katie's best friends, said. He placed his neon green snow saucer on the snow. "Let's make a chain."

"Cool," Katie agreed, lining her snow

saucer up behind Jeremy's and sitting down.

"Count me in!" Kevin told them. He lined his sled up behind Katie's saucer.

"Me too!" Emma Weber shouted, placing her sled behind Kevin's.

"Okay, everybody ready?" Jeremy shouted behind him.

"Oh yeah!" Katie exclaimed. "Let's go!"

A moment later, the train of sleds and saucers went zooming down the big hill on Surrey Lane. Katie loved sledding. It felt like she was flying without ever leaving the ground! Especially when she went down Surrey Lane—the steepest hill in town!

"Oh, that was a good one!" Jeremy exclaimed as they reached the bottom of the hill. "We went *so* fast."

"And I got it all on video," Suzanne Lock said, running over with a small video camera in her hand.

Katie grinned as Suzanne came closer. She was Katie's other best friend. Katie was glad

Suzanne wanted to go sledding, too. Except Suzanne didn't have a sled with her. All she had was her video camera.

"Where'd you get that?" Jeremy asked Suzanne.

"It was a gift from my uncle," Suzanne told him. "I just got it yesterday. I'm trying it out today."

"Cool!" Kevin exclaimed. "Did you get some shots of George going down the hill? He's amazing on that snowboard."

At just that moment, George went whizzing by.

"See what I mean?" Kevin asked.

"Yeah," Suzanne replied. But she didn't seem nearly as impressed as the other kids were. Instead, she turned her attention to Katie. "Will you tape me making a snow angel?"

Katie took the video camera from Suzanne's hands. "Sure," she said. "What do I do?"

"Just look through this little square. Once you can see me, press the red button," Suzanne said. Then she laid down in the snow and began moving her arms up and down.

"Got it," Katie said. She focused the camera on Suzanne and pushed the button.

"The trick to making a perfect snow angel is to move your arms and legs back and forth very slowly," Suzanne told Katie *and* the camera. "When you stand up, be sure not to make footprints inside the angel." She stood carefully, then leaped from her snow angel. Then she pointed toward the ground. "Ta-da! Perfect!"

"Ruff! Ruff! Arroooo!"

At just that moment, Pepper, Katie's chocolate-and-white cocker spaniel, came running across the snow. His best friend, Snowball, followed after him. The two dogs were chasing a gray squirrel.

"Oh, no!" Suzanne groaned as Pepper and Snowball ran right across her snow angel.

"Katie, look what your dumb dog and his friend did!"

That made Katie angry. Suzanne might be one of her best friends, but nobody—*nobody*—called Pepper dumb!

"He's smart!" Katie exclaimed. "He's just chasing a squirrel. That's what dogs do."

"Yeah, Suzanne," Jeremy said, jumping to Katie's defense. "And if you don't know that, then *you're* the one who's dumb!"

"Oh yeah?" Suzanne glared, completely forgetting Katie was still filming her. "Wanna bet?" She picked up a handful of snow and formed it into a ball. She chucked the snowball right at Jeremy.

"You asked for it!" Jeremy replied. He scooped up a snowball of his own and threw it at Suzanne.

"Snowball fight!" Kevin exclaimed happily.

"Yeah!" Emma W. cheered as she scooped up a big ball of snow.

"Make sure you keep the camera right on

me," Suzanne shouted to Katie. "I'm going to get Jeremy!"

Katie nodded. "Okay," she said. Then she bent down and started to pick up some snow with her free hand.

"No, Katie, don't!" Suzanne shouted. "You might get snow on my camera."

Katie frowned. She didn't want to be a cameraman. She wanted to take part in the snowball fight. "Here, take your . . ." she started to say to Suzanne. But before she could get the sentence out, Suzanne had taken off after Jeremy, with a snowball in her hand. There was nothing Katie could do but film the fight.

Still, that wasn't so bad. Especially when Jeremy, Kevin, and George all pelted Suzanne with snowballs at the same time.

Usually that would have upset Katie. She didn't like to see people ganging up on someone. But today Suzanne was being really bossy—even more so than usual.

✕ ✕ ✕

As soon as the snowball fight was over, Katie handed the video camera to Suzanne. She wanted to get back into the action.

"Wait for me!" Katie cried out as Emma W. and Kevin started to drag their sleds up the hill for another run.

"This is my last one," Kevin said. "I've

got snow in my hood and in my boots. Everywhere. Even in my underwear!"

Katie giggled. There was something about the word underwear that was just so funny!

"I'm getting pretty cold, too," Emma W. agreed.

"Why don't we go to my house for hot chocolate?" Katie invited her friends. "We've got the good kind with the little marsh-mallows in it."

"Cool," Jeremy said.

"No, *hot*!" George joked as he jumped onto his snowboard. "Meet you guys at the bottom of the hill! COWABUNGA!"

Chapter 2

"Hi, kids!" Mrs. Derkman waved as Katie and her friends walked by. "Having fun on your snow day?"

The kids all smiled and nodded. Then George said to Katie in a low voice, "I'll never get used to the fact that you live next door to a teacher. Especially *her*."

Katie knew what he meant. Mrs. Derkman had been their third-grade teacher. She was the strictest teacher in the whole school.

But outside of school, she wasn't strict at all. In fact, Mrs. Derkman could be kind of fun. Like right now, when she was building a snowman in her front yard.

"That's a really neat snowman, Mrs. Derkman," Emma W. said. "I like the flower necklace around its neck."

"And the grass skirt," Katie added.

"It's a Hawaiian snowwoman," Mrs. Derkman explained.

Katie giggled. That was probably the only Hawaiian snowwoman in the history of the world. After all, it never snowed in Hawaii.

Suzanne handed her camera to Katie. "Film me doing the hula next to the snowwoman," she told her.

"Suzanne, my fingers are frozen," Katie insisted. "I want to go inside for hot chocolate."

"Oh, come on. It'll just take a minute." Suzanne ran across Mrs. Derkman's front yard. Katie shrugged and pushed the red button on the camera.

Suzanne wiggled her hips and waved her arms back and forth and back and . . .

Oops! Suzanne knocked the head right off the snowwoman.

"Oh, Suzanne!" Mrs. Derkman exclaimed.

"Oops! Sorry," Suzanne apologized. "Do you want me to help you fix it?"

"I think you've done enough," Mrs. Derkman told Suzanne. "Go ahead inside and have hot chocolate with your friends."

Suzanne didn't have to be told twice. She turned and raced off. Katie and the other kids followed behind.

"Thanks for bringing Snowball home," Mrs. Derkman called over to Katie. "She fits right in with the snow, doesn't she?"

Katie grinned as the little white dog rolled around in the snow. Only her eyes and little black nose could be seen against the white background.

"Maybe you should build a snow *dog* next," Katie joked.

"Good idea!" Mrs. Derkman said. "Snowball the snowdog."

Katie smiled down at her own dog. "Come on, Pepper. Let's go inside and have a treat," she told him.

Pepper's tail began to wag wildly. He didn't understand a lot of people words. But he sure did understand *treat*.

✕ ✕ ✕

"Thank you for the hot chocolate, Mrs. Carew," Emma W. said to Katie's mother once they were all sitting in the warm kitchen. "I love the tiny marshmallows."

"Me too," George agreed. "And the cookies are awesome."

Katie grinned proudly. Her mother baked the best cookies in all of Cherrydale.

"I figured you kids would want some hot treats when you came inside," Katie's mother told them.

"I'm glad the mall was closed and you got the day off from work, Mom," Katie said.

"Me too," Mrs. Carew agreed. "I like going to work and being the manager of the Book Nook. But I really *love* snow days!"

"Who doesn't?" Jeremy piped up. "They're the best! I wish every day could be a snow day."

Oh, no. Not another wish.

Katie gasped. "No you don't!" she exclaimed. "You don't wish that at all."

The kids all stared at her curiously. Even Pepper cocked his head slightly and looked at her strangely.

Katie could tell they thought she was crazy. But she knew she wasn't. Every time the magic wind came, it switcherooed her into someone else. Still, she had to say something. The kids were all looking at her like she was nuts!

"I just mean that if every day were a snow day, we wouldn't think it was so special," Katie told them finally.

"That's true, Katie Kazoo," Emma W. agreed.

"What a wise thing to say," Katie's mother added.

"Well, *this* snow day sure was special," Suzanne piped up suddenly. "We all had a great time. And I got it all on tape. You guys want to watch it?"

"Sure," Katie said. "That'll be fun."

After helping to clean up their plates and

mugs, the kids all filed into Katie's living room. Suzanne connected her camera to the TV. Almost instantly, Suzanne's face appeared on the screen.

"It's a snow day!" Suzanne's voice rang out from the TV. "And my friends and I are having fun."

The scene switched to Suzanne making her snow angel.

"Man, this is boring," Kevin groaned while Suzanne gave her instructions for creating the perfect angel.

"This isn't a movie about *our* snow day," Jeremy complained. "It's all about you."

"No, you guys are in there, too," she insisted. "You're my supporting players."

"Oh, give me a break!" George sighed. "You didn't get one shot of me on my snowboard. And I was really rocking out there!"

"You sure were," Kevin agreed.

A moment later, the scene switched again. Once again, Suzanne was right in the middle of the picture. But this time she was being pelted with snowballs from every direction. Worse yet, her nose was running.

"Eew! Suzanne's got a booger!" George groaned.

"Katie!" Suzanne shouted. "Why would you film that?"

"You told me to keep the camera right on you," Katie said. "So I did. I didn't realize your nose was running."

"This is hilarious," George said. He practically fell off his chair, he was laughing so hard.

"Wait, it gets better," Kevin said, watching Suzanne's hula dance in Mrs. Derkman's yard. "Plop . . . there goes the snowwoman's head."

"This is the best comedy I've ever seen," Jeremy agreed. "Better than anything on TV."

Suzanne frowned. "I'm glad I could entertain all of you."

Suddenly, Katie felt bad for her best friend. She really wanted to cheer her up. "That's exactly what you did, Suzanne," she said sincerely. "You entertained us. Like a real actress in a funny movie."

Suzanne brightened slightly. "Yeah. I guess I did. I was pretty hilarious, wasn't I? It's amazing just how much the camera loves me."

"Oh, give me a break!" George complained. "Suzanne, you are so stuck-up."

But Suzanne didn't hear a word he said. She was too busy admiring herself on the screen.

Chapter 3

When Katie woke up in the morning, she was glad to see that the sun was shining. That meant there would be school. She was also happy to see that Jeremy's wish had not come true.

But there was still plenty of snow. And sure enough, by the time Katie arrived at school, the whole playground was filled with kids throwing snowballs and building snowmen. Katie watched George snowboard down a small hill in the field behind school.

"You're looking really good on that thing," Katie shouted to him.

George waved and ran up to her. "These

aren't as steep or as much fun as the big hill on Surrey Lane," George complained.

"You really like snowboarding, don't you?" Katie asked.

"Totally!" George exclaimed. "I'm going to be the next Tony Raven!"

"Tony who?" Katie asked.

"You've never heard of Tony *Raven*?" George sounded amazed. "He's the number one snowboarder in the whole world."

"Oh," Katie said.

"Well, you're going to hear a lot about him soon," George continued. "He's coming to Cherrydale to make a commercial for Winter Wildness Clothing."

Just then, Emma Stavros walked by. She stopped when she heard George talking about Tony Raven. "He's not the only one who's going to be in those commercials," she told him. "Kerry Gaffigan is, too. Tony's her boyfriend. And she's the other spokesperson for Winter Wildness."

"Yeah, well, it's Tony who is going to sell those clothes," George insisted. "Everyone wants to be like him."

"I don't," Emma S. insisted. "I'd much rather be like Kerry."

"Maybe that's why they're doing the commercial together," Katie suggested, trying to stop an argument before it started.

"Huh?" George and Emma S. asked at the same time.

"That way men and women will both buy Winter Wildness clothing," Katie explained.

George shrugged. "I guess. Anyway, all I know is that there is a huge party on Saturday to celebrate the new clothes. It's going to be right here in Cherrydale. And I plan to be there."

By this time, a group of kids had gathered around George, Emma S., and Katie. At the sound of the words "big party," they all got really interested.

All except Suzanne. She seemed kind of

bored by the whole thing. At least until she heard Emma S. say, "Yeah. They're going to have a red carpet, celebrities, and all kinds of reporters and photographers and stuff."

"Did somebody say *red carpet*?" Suzanne piped up enthusiastically.

George rolled his eyes. He knew what Suzanne was thinking. They all did.

"Yeah, but only Tony, Kerry, and other celebrities are going to be walking on it," George told Suzanne. "The rest of us will have to stand behind a rope or something."

"Where is the red carpet going to be?" Suzanne asked.

"Near Surrey Lane," Emma S. told her.

"Tony's going to snowboard down the big hill, leap over a mogul, and land at the edge of the carpet," George explained.

"Where Kerry will be waiting for him," Emma S. added.

"That sounds so romantic," Becky Stern cooed. "Doesn't it, Jeremy?"

Jeremy rolled his eyes and groaned. So did George and Kevin.

"What's a mogul?" Katie asked, changing the subject.

"It's a huge lump of hard, icy snow on a ski slope," George told her. "It's really hard to snowboard over one."

"Tony Raven can do it, though, right?" Jeremy asked.

"Tony Raven can do anything!" George exclaimed. "It's going to be so exciting to see him in person."

"Totally!" Kevin agreed. "Are you going to get his autograph, George?"

"I'm gonna try," George replied.

"I already have Kerry's autograph," Emma S. boasted.

"I want to get autographs from both of them," Zoe Canter said. "I wasn't able to go to Kerry's show last week."

"Do you think we'll get anywhere near Tony and Kerry?" Jeremy wondered.

"We can try," Katie told him. "Bring your camera. At least we can get their photographs."

Miriam turned to Suzanne. "Do you want Kerry and Tony's autographs?" she asked her.

Suzanne shook her head. "Celebrities don't ask other celebrities for autographs," she said. "It's tacky."

Suzanne, a celebrity? Katie rolled her eyes, but she didn't say anything.

George had plenty to say, though. "You're not a celebrity, Suzanne. You're a normal kid, just like the rest of us."

"Suzanne's not normal, George," Kevin disagreed.

Suzanne began to smile proudly. She was obviously glad someone recognized what a star she was.

But then Kevin added, "She's *weirder* than the rest of us."

The boys all started to laugh.

Katie gulped. She had a feeling that was

going to make Suzanne really angry. And when Suzanne got angry, Suzanne got mean!

But surprisingly, Suzanne didn't get angry at all. In fact, she gave Kevin a big smile. "Maybe I'm not a celebrity yet," she told him. "But by the time that party rolls around, I will be. We'll see who's laughing then!"

Chapter 4

It took a really long time for the kids in class 4A to get settled that morning. By the time they'd taken off their boots, hung up their coats, and made sure no one had misplaced their hats, it seemed like half the morning had gone by.

But that didn't stop Mr. Guthrie from teaching. He waited until everyone was sitting in their beanbags. Then he showered them with snow. Well, not real snow. Paper snow. And each flake was different. Just like real snowflakes.

"Let me guess," Kevin said. "Today we're going to be learning about snow."

Mr. G. nodded. "Good guess, Kev-o," he answered. "Today we're going to find out how and where snow is created in the atmosphere. But not right away."

Katie picked up one of the paper snowflakes Mr. G. had tossed around the classroom. The flake had something written on it in icy silver letters.

"Frostbite," Katie read out loud. She looked up at Mr. G. "What's that supposed to mean?" she asked her teacher.

"It's the answer to a riddle," Mr. G. explained to her. "The question is written on one of the other snowflakes. Can anyone find it?"

The kids all started picking up flakes. "I've got it!" Mandy told Katie excitedly. She looked down at her piece of carefully cut white paper and read, "What do you get if you mix an icicle and a shark?"

"Frostbite," Katie repeated. She giggled. "Now I get it."

"Okay, listen to this one," George shouted out, holding up a snowflake. "What do snowmen wear on their heads?" he read.

"Ice caps!" Andy replied, holding up his snowflake.

"This is the best joke off we've ever had, because we're all a part of it," Emma S. said.

Katie knew just what she meant. Usually it was only George and Kadeem who told jokes in the classroom. But today everyone had a chance.

"Who's got the answer to this riddle?" Emma S. asked. "How do you know if there's been a snowman in your bed?"

"You wake up wet!" Kadeem called from across the room. He waved his paper snowflake in the air.

Emma W. bent down and picked up a paper snowflake. "By icicle," she read aloud.

"That's the answer to my riddle," Kevin told her. "How do snowmen travel around?"

"By icicle," Emma W. repeated. She looked confused, then smiled. "Now I get it! *By i*cicle instead of *bi*cycle."

This game sure was a lot of fun.

"What sort of ball doesn't bounce?" the teacher read from a snowflake.

"A snowball!" Emma S. told him. "I didn't even need a snowflake to know the answer. It's an old riddle."

"Here's another one," George called out.

"What did the hat say to the scarf?"

Kevin held up a new snowflake. "You hang around while I go on a head!" he answered.

George and Kevin both laughed really, really hard.

"That was a good one!" George exclaimed. "I'll have to remember it."

Katie really loved being in class 4A. Mr. G. always made sure that school was exciting. Everything they did was just a little bit wacky. And that made learning fun.

She grinned. Even though it was freezing outside, being in her classroom gave her a nice warm feeling inside.

Chapter 5

"Did you know that snow is made of dirt and ice?" Kevin asked Jeremy as the kids sat down in the cafeteria at lunchtime.

"Every snowflake has six sides," Katie added.

"And as snow falls, the flakes join together to make bigger flakes," Emma S. said.

"I guess you guys were learning about snow in class today," Jeremy said.

"Oh yeah," George told him. "And we also learned where snowmen go to dance."

"Where?" Miriam asked him.

"Snow *balls*!" George said. Then he started laughing. "That was one of the jokes Mr. G. taught us."

"Mr. G. is teaching you jokes now?" Suzanne asked. "Why would he do that?"

"To make class fun," Katie told her. "He always does stuff like that."

Suzanne shook her head and sighed. "You guys have the weirdest classroom," she said.

Katie sighed. She knew Suzanne was just jealous. She also knew Suzanne would never admit it.

"Hey, you guys want to build a snow fort on the field during recess?" Jeremy asked.

"Totally!" Kevin exclaimed.

"That sounds like fun," Emma S. agreed.

"And we could build a snowman soldier to defend the fort," George suggested.

"I'm really good at building snowmen," Becky told him. She picked up the banana from her tray. "This can be the nose."

Katie opened her mouth to speak, but Suzanne stopped her. "Katie and I can't help you. We already have something planned for recess," Suzanne said.

"We do?" Katie asked. She had no idea what Suzanne was talking about.

Suzanne pulled her video camera from her coat pocket. "We're going to make a sportswear commercial. I'm going to be the star. I'll talk about my gorgeous pink parka while you follow me around the yard."

Katie frowned. She did *not* want to spend recess walking around the playground filming Suzanne. "Come on, Suzanne," she told her friend, trying not to sound too mean. "I'd rather help build a snow fort."

"But Katie, I *need* you," Suzanne pleaded. "I'm making an audition tape to give to the director of Tony and Kerry's commercial. How can I do that all by myself?"

Katie didn't know the answer to that one.

"I think you should be the director *and* the

camera operator," Suzanne told Katie. "And we'll give you full credit on the tape. It will say 'directed by Katie Carew.'"

Katie thought about that. Suzanne had said Katie would be the director. That would mean she would be giving the orders for a change.

"Okay," Katie agreed finally. "But just this one time."

"Sure," Suzanne said. "We can make the whole commercial in one recess. After all, I'm a professional."

George, Kevin, and Jeremy all started to giggle. George laughed so hard, chocolate pudding came out of his nose.

Suzanne scowled. "Come on, Katie. We need to get started now," she said, ignoring the boys.

"But I'm not finished with . . ." Katie began, pointing to her dessert.

"There's no time for brownies now," Suzanne said. "We have a lot of work to do on my audition tape."

Katie sighed. *So much for being in charge.* She took another bite of brownie, put on her coat, and followed Suzanne out onto the playground.

Chapter 6

When Katie woke up the next morning, it was snowing again. Hard.

Really, *really* hard.

Snow day hard.

Quickly, Katie scrambled out of bed and went down to the kitchen in her pajamas. There was no reason to get dressed if there was going to be a snow day.

Of course, Katie didn't know for sure yet. It wouldn't be official until a snow day was announced on the radio.

"Did they say if the Cherrydale schools are closed?" Katie asked her dad as she walked into the kitchen.

Mr. Carew shook his head. "They haven't read the school closings yet. I think they'll announce them after this commercial."

Katie sat impatiently at the kitchen table and listened along with her mom and dad. The commercial—something about a new brand of air freshener—seemed to go on forever. And then, finally, the announcer came on.

"And now for the school closings in our area . . ." he began.

Katie crossed her fingers and toes really tight for luck.

"Schools will be closed in Apple Valley, Brighton Bay, Carlton County, Cherrydale . . ."

Katie leaped up as the announcer read the name of her town. "You heard it!" she said to her parents. "He said Cherrydale. It's another snow day for me!"

"Ruff! Ruff!" Pepper started to bark. His stubby little tail wagged back and forth. He had no idea what was happening, of course. But just hearing Katie so happy made him happy, too!

Rrringg . . . A minute later, the phone rang. Katie rushed over and picked it up.

"Did you hear? We have a snow day!"

Katie giggled. "Hi to you, too, Jeremy," she said.

"Oh, yeah. Hi, Katie Kazoo," Jeremy corrected himself. "Do you want to go sledding?"

"Definitely," Katie said.

"Cool. Meet me at the big hill on Surrey Lane at ten o'clock," Jeremy said. "I'll call Andy, Manny, George, and Kevin."

"And I'll call some of the girls," Katie assured him.

"Great. See you there," Jeremy said.

Katie grinned as she hung up the phone. This was going to be a great day.

✕　✕　✕

Or maybe not.

SURREY LANE CLOSED.

That was what the sign said when Katie and her friends arrived at the big hill. There were ropes blocking the hill from traffic, and policemen were all around. In the distance, Katie could see workers putting up a big tent.

"Sorry, kids," one of the policemen told them. "You're going to have to sled somewhere else today."

"But this is the best hill in the whole town!" Jeremy insisted. "No place else is as steep."

The policeman nodded. "I know," he said kindly. "But we had to block it off so they can get ready for Saturday's big party."

"I know all about that," George told the policeman. "Tony Raven, the snowboarder, will be on the red carpet."

"Yep," the policeman said.

"Look!" Jeremy said. "He just pulled up in the white limo over there!"

George gasped. His face turned as white as the snow on the ground.

The policeman stared at George. "What's the matter with him?" he asked Katie.

"Nothing," Katie replied. "He just can't

believe he's standing so close to his hero."

"I'm going to ask Tony to autograph my snowboard," George said when he was finally able to speak. And with that, George ran off toward the limousine.

But he didn't get very far. Katie could see one of Tony Raven's bodyguards stopping him.

"You can't come over here, kid," he said.

"But I just want Tony to sign my board," George explained. He held up his snowboard.

"Not now, kid," the bodyguard insisted.

Katie and her friends all watched as Tony climbed out of the car, stood up, and walked away, without ever looking in George's direction.

Katie felt awful for her friend. His hero had just ignored him. She hurried over and stood by George's side.

"That was so mean," she told George.

George shrugged. "He didn't even say hello," he murmured, sounding like he might cry.

"That stinks," Andy told him.

"I can't believe Kerry Gaffigan would have a boyfriend like that," Emma S. added.

"When I'm a celebrity, I'll sign my autograph for you, George," Suzanne assured him. "No matter how many times you ask."

The kids all stared at her.

"What?" Suzanne asked them. "I was just trying to make him feel better."

Katie turned her attention back to George. "You know what?" she asked him. "Tony Raven doesn't deserve a fan like you, George. He's a big jerk."

"Whatever," George said sadly.

"And just for that, none of us are ever going to buy Winter Wildness clothing, *ever*!" Katie exclaimed.

Katie must have shouted really loudly, because just then a man in a dark gray wool coat looked in her direction. Then he walked over toward where Tony Raven was standing.

The man began talking angrily at Tony. Tony Raven turned in Katie's direction. His eyes were all squinty and small. He looked mad.

Katie figured it was a good time to get out of there. "You guys, I'm cold," she told her friends.

"Why don't we all go to my house?" Suzanne suggested.

"Sure," Katie said.

"Why not?" Jeremy agreed.

"I've got nothing else to do," George said sadly. "I don't feel like finding another hill and snowboarding, anyhow."

"Great!" Suzanne exclaimed. "We can watch a tape. And I know the perfect one."

Katie didn't like the sound of that. Neither did the other kids. They all could guess just what movie Suzanne was talking about—the commercial she and Katie had been making at recess yesterday.

"You know what?" Jeremy said suddenly. "I just remembered that I have homework to do."

"Me too," Emma S. said. "I better get going."

"Yeah, I think I hear my mother calling me," George said.

"You live four blocks away, George," Suzanne said.

"I have really great ears," George said, running off before Suzanne could question him further.

A moment later, Katie and Suzanne were standing all by themselves. Suzanne looked curiously at Katie. "Was it something I said?" she asked.

Chapter 7

On Saturday night, Cherrydale's Surrey
Lane looked like it could be the Academy
Awards. A red carpet led from the street to the
tent at the foot of the hill. Spotlights shone so
brightly, you could see them from anywhere in
town. And there were photographers. Lots and
lots of photographers.

"Kerry, look over here!" one cameraman
shouted as Kerry Gaffigan walked across the
red carpet in a bright yellow Winter Wildness
ski jacket and snow pants.

"Kerry, turn around and give me a smile!"
screamed another.

"Kerry, when is Tony making his big

entrance?" a third photographer asked.

Tony Raven hadn't arrived yet, but just about everyone else in town was there. They were all waiting to see Tony Raven snowboard down the big hill and stop right where his girlfriend, Kerry Gaffigan, was standing.

Even if Tony Raven was a jerk, Katie couldn't help being excited. After all, stuff like this didn't happen every day in Cherrydale.

"When the man who is going to be directing the commercial walks onto the red carpet, I'm going to rush up there and give him my commercial tape," Suzanne explained to Katie.

Katie frowned.

"I mean *our* commercial tape," Suzanne corrected herself.

"They're not going to let you anywhere near that red carpet," Katie told her.

"Why not? I heard there are going to be *lots* of models here," Suzanne said.

"*Real* models, Suzanne," Katie told her. "Not kids who are taking modeling lessons."

"I *am* a real model," Suzanne insisted. "I just haven't gotten my big break yet."

Katie rolled her eyes. There was no use arguing with Suzanne. Besides, she didn't want to ruin such an exciting night with a fight. This was a once in a lifetime event.

And George was missing it. He was still mad at Tony Raven. Katie understood how he felt, but she hated the idea that her pal wasn't here at this big event. He was really going to regret it on Monday when everyone in school was talking about it.

Katie couldn't let that happen! She turned suddenly, and started walking toward the edge of the crowd.

"Where are you going?" Suzanne called after her.

"To get George," Katie said. "Don't worry, I'll be back way before Tony Raven snowboards over that mogul!"

✕ ✕ ✕

✕

Within a few minutes, Katie had made it to George's block. The street was completely empty. That wasn't surprising. Everyone was at Surrey Lane. George was probably the only kid in town who was still home.

Just then, Katie felt a winter breeze blow on the back of her neck. Whew. It was getting really cold out here. She pulled her long

green scarf tighter around her neck.

But a wool scarf wasn't going to block out this wind. This was the *magic* wind. Nothing could stop it.

The magic wind picked up speed, circling wildly around Katie. It was so cold and powerful, Katie thought she might be blown away. She shut her eyes tight and tried not to cry.

And then it stopped. Just like that.

The magic wind was gone, and so was Katie Carew.

She'd been turned into someone else.

But who?

Chapter 8

Katie slowly opened her eyes. Everything was kind of blurry. She blinked a few times, and then squinted to see where she was.

Whoa! Wherever she was, she was sure up high. Down below, she could just about make out a white tent and a red carpet.

The magic wind had blown Katie straight to the top of the big hill near Surrey Lane. Okay, so now Katie knew *where* she was. But she still didn't know *who* she was. Katie glanced down at her feet. Her green winter boots had been replaced with a pair of thick red-and-yellow ski boots.

Her winter jacket was gone, too. Instead,

she was wearing a red and yellow ski coat. The words *Winter Wildness* were written like graffiti going down the sleeve.

Katie had never seen these clothes before in her life.

At just that moment, she spotted the bright yellow, orange, and red snowboard lying by her feet on the snow. Katie had never seen a snowboard like this one. For starters, it was much bigger than George's. It was definitely a grown-up's board.

There was also something written on the board. Katie tried to read it, but the words looked all blurry. She picked up the board and held it close to her face so she could read it.

PROPERTY OF TONY RAVEN.

Katie gulped. That could only mean one thing. The magic wind had switcherooed her into Tony Raven, champion snowboarder.

That meant all those people down there were waiting for her to come speeding down the mountain on that snowboard.

Not only that, they expected her to leap over some giant frozen snow lump. What was it George had called it? Oh yeah. A mogul. And if Katie remembered correctly, George had said that was really hard to do . . . especially for someone who had never been on a snowboard in her life.

Except Katie wasn't Katie right now. She was Tony Raven. And all those people down there were expecting her to snowboard down to them.

This was soooo not good!

Suddenly Katie heard loud music blaring down below. It sounded like a huge marching band was playing. Then she heard a man's voice over the loudspeaker.

"Ladies and gentlemen, here he comes! Tony Raven!"

Katie knew that meant she was supposed to get on Tony's snowboard and glide down the big hill. But she felt as frozen as an icicle. She could just imagine the newspapers tomorrow. There would be big stories about Tony Raven being too chicken to snowboard down Surrey Lane. People would be laughing at him.

Katie thought about that. Maybe Tony deserved to be laughed at. After all, Tony wasn't a very nice man. Look at how he'd ignored George.

She shook her head. *No.* No matter what, two wrongs didn't make a right.

"Here comes Tony Raven!" the man with the loudspeaker announced again, louder this time.

In the distance, Katie could hear the crowd cheering. She squinted. The crowd was just a big blur. "Tony! Tony! Tony!" They sounded really excited.

"Hey, Tony, can you hear us up there?" the man with the loudspeaker called up to Katie. "Kerry's waiting for you. We're all waiting for you!"

Why did he have to say that? Katie took a

big gulp. There was only one way she could get down that hill.

Hey! Wait a minute! Suddenly Katie had a great idea! Well, maybe not great. But an idea, at least!

Chapter 9

"WHEEEEE!" Katie shouted loudly as she whooshed down the big hill at top speed. She held on tight to the snowboard.

What were the reporters and fans going to think, seeing Tony Raven sitting—instead of standing—on his snowboard? They were probably going to be disappointed. But they'd be even more disappointed if he never arrived at the red carpet.

Everything was a blur around Katie as she slid down the giant hill. In a way, Katie figured that was a good thing. It would be even scarier if she knew when that big mogul was coming. At least this way she'd be surprised.

"YIKES!" Katie screamed out as the snow-board came in contact with the big icy bump!

"HELP!" Katie cried even louder as the snowboard took off into the air. Katie looked down. The ground seemed far, far away. Snow shot out from beneath the board, blowing around her head, in her mouth, and even up her nose.

Katie was flying . . . actually flying! "AAAHHHH!" she cried out.

Thump! And then she landed, *hard*. The snow below may have looked soft, but it was no pillow. *Ooh*. Her rear end was going to be sore tomorrow.

The snowboard picked up speed, zooming down the hill faster and faster, as though it were sliding down a sheet of ice. Now Katie could kind of make out a squiggly line of red getting closer. It had to be the red carpet.

The board coasted to a stop as the ground flattened out. Katie took a deep breath, and then struggled to her feet.

Flashbulbs began popping everywhere. The lights were blinding. Katie couldn't see a thing. But she could *hear*. And the sounds coming into her ears were not very nice.

"BOOOO!" the crowd shouted in her direction.

"You stink!" a kid cried out.

"Tony Raven is a wimp!" another insisted.

Then Katie heard a familiar voice beside her on the red carpet.

"I can't believe you did that, Tony!" Kerry Gaffigan said. "I'm so embarrassed!"

Katie felt terrible. She'd done the best she could. She'd made it all the way down the mountain and over that big mogul. Flying through the air like that had been really scary. But it *still* hadn't been enough to please the crowd, or Kerry Gaffigan.

Katie could feel the tears welling up in her eyes. She was going to cry. Then all the photographers would have pictures of Tony Raven crying like a fourth-grade girl.

Katie had done enough to Tony Raven. She couldn't let that happen, too. She turned quickly and ran as fast as she could off the red carpet—past the crowd and into the dark, lonely streets of Cherrydale.

The sound of the booing crowd grew fainter as Katie got farther away. She was happy about that. Having people boo at her—even if it wasn't really her they were booing—really hurt her feelings.

Just then, Katie felt a cold breeze blowing against the back of her neck. A second later, the breeze picked up speed, blowing faster and faster until it turned into a tornado. A tornado just around Katie.

The magic wind was back.

Katie grabbed onto a nearby lamppost to keep from being blown away. She shut her eyes and tried not to cry as the wind whistled louder and louder.

And then it stopped. Just like that. Switcheroo! She was back to being Katie Kazoo.

Tony Raven was back to his old self, too. He was standing next to her. And boy, did he look confused.

"Hey, where am I?" he asked, squinting his eyes and looking around. "And who are you?"

"You're on Nightingale Road," Katie told him. "And I'm Katie Carew."

"Nice to meet you," Tony said. He shook his head as he tried to make sense of things. "I don't think I'm supposed to be here. I'm supposed to be on the red carpet right now."

Katie kicked at the ground with her green boot. "Uh . . . um . . . you were already there," she told him. "You kinda ran off."

"Ran off? Why?" he asked. Then he stopped for a minute and thought. "Oh, no. Why do I have a feeling that I went down that hill on my rear end?"

Katie frowned. "Because you did," she told him.

"But why would I do that?" Tony asked.

"Maybe you were afraid of that big mogul," Katie suggested.

Tony shook his head. "That little bump? That's nothing for me. At least, not usually. Something seems to be kind of wrong with me tonight. Maybe I'm getting sick."

Katie sighed. She knew that wasn't it at all. But she also knew she could never tell Tony the truth. He wouldn't believe it.

"I think I need to lie down," he said. "Do you know how to get to the Cherrydale Inn? That's where I'm staying."

"It's just two blocks to the left," Katie told him.

"Would you mind walking there with me?" Tony asked her. "I'm not wearing my glasses. I can't see too well without them. I'm liable to get lost."

Well, that explained why everything had been so blurry, Katie thought. Wait! Did that also explain why Tony had acted as though he didn't even see George the other day? Maybe it did! Tony Raven hadn't been wearing glasses then, either. He wasn't mean after all!

"Why aren't you wearing your glasses?" Katie asked him.

"I don't like how they look in pictures," Tony admitted. "So I don't wear them when there are photographers around."

"That's silly," Katie told him. "Glasses are totally cool. My friend Jeremy wears them and he's the best athlete in the school. If he didn't wear his glasses, he'd never be able to see a soccer ball or hit a baseball. If you wore *your* glasses, you'd be able to see all your fans smiling at you."

Tony nodded. "I know," he admitted. "Kerry tells me that all the time. And she keeps trying to bug me to get contact lenses. But I'm afraid to put them in my eyes."

Katie tried not to laugh. Tony Raven wasn't afraid to fly over a mogul on a high mountain, but he was too chicken to wear contact lenses. How silly was that?

"I'll help you get to the inn," Katie told him.

"Thanks," Tony said. "I really need to get some rest. I'm going to have a lot of explaining to do tomorrow." He paused for a minute and shook his head. "And I don't have the faintest idea what I'm going to say."

Chapter 10

RAVEN TURNS CHICKEN!

That was the headline in the newspaper the next morning. Katie turned beet red as she looked at the picture of Tony Raven sliding down the hill on his rear end. She was really embarrassed. After all, she knew it wasn't Tony, but Katie Carew who had turned chicken.

Rrringg. Katie jumped up from the breakfast table to answer the telephone. "Hello?" she said.

"Hey, Katie Kazoo," George said. "Did you see today's paper?"

"Yes," Katie said sadly. "Isn't it awful?"

"Awful?" George asked. "Are you nuts? I think it's great."

"But everybody is making fun of Tony Raven," Katie insisted.

"It serves him right for being such a snob," George told her. "I can't believe I ever liked him."

"He wasn't being a snob that day, George," Katie insisted. "He couldn't see you. He can't see *anything* without his glasses on. Everything's all blurry."

"How do you know that?" George asked.

Oops. "I . . . uh . . . I read it somewhere," Katie said.

"Well, whatever," George said. "Anyway, after this, I bet his career is over. It says in the newspaper that Winter Wildness Clothing wants to cancel his contract because of what happened."

Now Katie felt really awful. She couldn't let that happen. She had to do something. But what?

"I just don't understand what made Tony Raven act like that," George continued. "I mean, why would he go down that hill like a kid on a sled?"

Katie's eyes popped open wide. That was it!

"George, I gotta go," she said. "There's something I really have to do!"

✕　✕　✕

A few minutes later, Katie was dressed and heading down the block to the Cherrydale Inn. It was only a few blocks from her house, but Katie would have to move really fast. She had to arrive before Tony Raven left town.

"Tony, wait!" Katie shouted as she raced up to the inn. The snowboarder was getting into a limousine with Kerry Gaffigan and another man.

"Oh, it's you," Tony said as soon as Katie came into view.

"Hi," Katie greeted him. "I like your glasses."

"Thanks," Tony said. "I'm going to wear them from now on."

"That's great," Katie told him.

Tony turned to Kerry and the other man. "This is Katie, the girl who helped me find my way back here last night," he introduced her. "Katie, this is Kerry and RJ. RJ is the owner of the Winter Wildness Clothing Company."

"We've met," Kerry said. "Katie was at my ice-skating show."

Katie couldn't believe that someone as famous as Kerry Gaffigan actually remembered her. But Katie couldn't think about that now.

"I just wanted to tell you how great you were last night," she said to Tony.

Tony, Kerry, and RJ all looked at her with surprise.

"Great?" RJ asked. "Are you kidding?"

Katie shook her head. "My parents thought he was great, too. They thought it was cool how

Tony showed that Winter Wildness clothing brings out the kid in everyone."

"Huh?" Tony and Kerry said at once.

RJ was scratching his forehead. "Hmm. Not a bad line . . . 'Winter Wildness—let our clothes bring out the kid in you.'"

"Exactly," Katie continued. "My mom and dad hate snow. To them, it just means a lot of shoveling. But last night Tony showed grown-ups that if they put on Winter Wildness clothes, they'll want to get outdoors in the snow, just like when they were kids . . . at

least, that's what my parents said."

"Was that what you were doing, Tony?" RJ asked him. "Starting your own ad campaign?"

"Well . . . I . . . uh . . ." Tony obviously didn't know what to say.

"Of course he was," Katie answered for him. "Couldn't you tell?"

"Why didn't you say anything about it?" Kerry asked Tony.

"Maybe he wanted it to be a surprise," Katie said.

"Yeah, yeah, I wanted it to be a surprise," Tony echoed.

Katie giggled. It was even a surprise to Tony.

"I like this idea," RJ said. "I think we should go with it."

"You do?" Tony asked. "Um . . . I mean, of course you do. It's a good idea." He winked at Katie. She winked back.

"In fact, I think we should start a line of kids clothing, too," RJ added.

"Good thinking, RJ." Tony paused for a minute. "I have another idea. We should have lots of kids in the commercial with us." He smiled at Katie. "Do you know any kids who might want to be in it?"

Katie grinned back at him. Did she *ever*!

Chapter 11

"There I am!" George shouted. "Look at me coming down that mountain next to Tony!"

The kids all stared at the TV screen in Katie's living room. Two weeks had passed since they had helped make the Winter Wildness Clothing commercial. They were watching it now for the first time.

"Wow!" Katie exclaimed as she saw Tony take on a big mogul.

"And there I am, skating on the ice, right next to Kerry," Emma S. squealed.

"Oooh, I see us, Katie!" Jeremy shouted.

Katie smiled. Sure enough, there she was, having a snowball fight with Jeremy, Kerry, and Tony. They were on TV!

"There's Miriam, Emma W., and me having hot chocolate with Tony Raven and Kerry Gaffigan," Kevin shouted excitedly.

"I'll bet my snow angel scene is next," Suzanne boasted. "I was the most professional actor there. The director is definitely going to want to end the commercial with the best performer."

The kids all rolled their eyes.

"Yep, here I come," Suzanne said. "That's the pink and white parka I was wearing." Sure enough, a pink and white ski jacket came into focus on the screen. "Wait until you guys see how beautiful I look on camera."

The camera closed in on the sleeve of Suzanne's jacket, where the words *Winter Wildness* were written.

Then the announcer said, "Winter Wildness Clothing. It will bring out the kid in you."

And that was it. The commercial was over.

Katie glanced over at her best friend. Poor

Suzanne. They'd never even shown her face!

Nobody said anything for a minute. They all felt too bad for Suzanne. The kids knew exactly what she had to be thinking.

A second later, it was Suzanne who broke the silence. "The point of a commercial is to sell the product," she said confidently. "Any real model knows that. You could see the words *Winter Wildness* clearly on my sleeve. It's what people will remember. *My* part in the commercial was the most important!"

Katie choked back a laugh. Suzanne would never change.

Still, sometimes it was good when things stayed the same. Especially since sooner or later, the magic wind would come back, and then *everything* would change for Katie Kazoo. One, two . . . switcheroo!

About the Author

NANCY KRULIK is the author of more than 150 books for children and young adults, including three *New York Times* bestsellers. She lives in New York City with her husband, composer Daniel Burwasser, their children, Amanda and Ian, and Pepper, a chocolate and white spaniel mix. When she's not busy writing the *Katie Kazoo, Switcheroo* series, Nancy loves swimming, reading, and going to the movies.

About the Illustrators

JOHN & WENDY'S art has been featured in other books for children, in magazines, on stationery, and on toys. When they are not drawing Katie and her friends, they like to paint, take photographs, travel, and play music in their rock 'n' roll band. They live and work in Brooklyn, New York.